The Baddies

By Julia Donaldson and illustrated by Axel Scheffler

Scholastic Press • New York

There once lived a troll and a ghost and a witch.
They were horrible baddies all three.
They never said sorry or thank you or please,
And their hearts were as hard as could be.

And the worst thing about the three baddies
(The troll and the witch and the ghost)
Was the fact that all three of them *liked* being bad,
And what's more, they all liked to boast.

The troll said,
    "I'm stronger than you two.
I can easily win every fight."

The ghost said,
    "I'm much the most scary.
I make things go bump in the night."

The witch said, "My magic
    turns men into mice
And rubies and pearls into coal,
So you'd better beware,
    or you'll end up as frogs,
Or maybe as toads-in-the-hole."

When a girl with a blue spotted hanky
Moved into a cottage nearby,
The witch rubbed her hands
  and the troll roared with joy
And the ghost gave a long happy sigh.

The ghost said, "I can't wait to haunt her
Until she's a quivering jelly."
The troll said, "I'm going to eat her,"
And he patted his big bulgy belly.

"Before you can try,
  I'll have turned her to stone!"
Cried the witch, in a voice loud and shrill.
"Oh no you won't!" yelled the others,
And the witch replied, "Oh yes I will!"

The three of them started to quarrel,
And before very long they were fighting.
There was pushing and shoving
  and pulling of hair.
There was pinching and kicking and biting!

"Enough!" squeaked a mouse
who had heard every word.
"Let's find out who's really the worst.
Could anyone steal the girl's hanky?
I wonder who'd like to go first?"

"Me!" roared the troll, ducking under a bridge.
"Just wait till she crosses this stream.
I'll pop up and seize that blue hanky,
And I'll ROAR till you all hear her scream."

So he hid
and he waited,

then popped up and
roared,

But the girl didn't tremble or yell.
She just did a neat little sidestep,
And the troll lost his balance and fell.

He ended up
- **splash** -
in the water,

And the other two laughed, "Tee-hee-hee!"
The girl trotted off with her hanky,
And the troll was as wet as could be.

"Me next!" cried the witch,
    and she looked up a spell
To magic things out of a pocket.

"Hankety pankety
plinkety plonk,
Rickety rackety rocket!"

She chanted the spell with a wave of her wand,
And from the girl's pocket there flew
A toffee, some string and a worm, while the girl
Sneezed into her hanky, **"Ah-choo!"**

The toffee got stuck to the witch's long nose,
And the string tangled up round her knee.
So the girl kept the blue spotted hanky,
And the witch went as red as could be.

"My turn," said the ghost with a giggle.
"I'll hover around till it's night.
Then I'll glide through the wall of her bedroom
And give her a terrible fright.
I'll moan and I'll groan and I'll rattle my chains
Till she howls and she wails (just like me).

"Then I'll sidle away
with the hanky
And leave her as
scared as can be."

But when he appeared
in her bedroom . . .

The girl said, "Poor ghost, can't you sleep?
Perhaps a hot bath would be helpful,
Or else you could try counting sheep?"

She read him a couple of stories
And made him a nice cup of tea,

Then she waved him good-bye
with her hanky,
And the ghost was as cross
as could be.

Next morning the girl
washed her hanky.

Then she spotted the little white mouse
Who squeaked, "Can you please help my babies?
It's terribly cold in our house."

The little girl thought for a moment,
And on the next page you will see . . .

That the mice got the blue spotted hanky,
And they were as snug as could be.

So the baddies
  were soundly defeated,
And they said to each other,
  "Let's pack."

Then they went off to stay with an ogre,
And none of them ever came back.

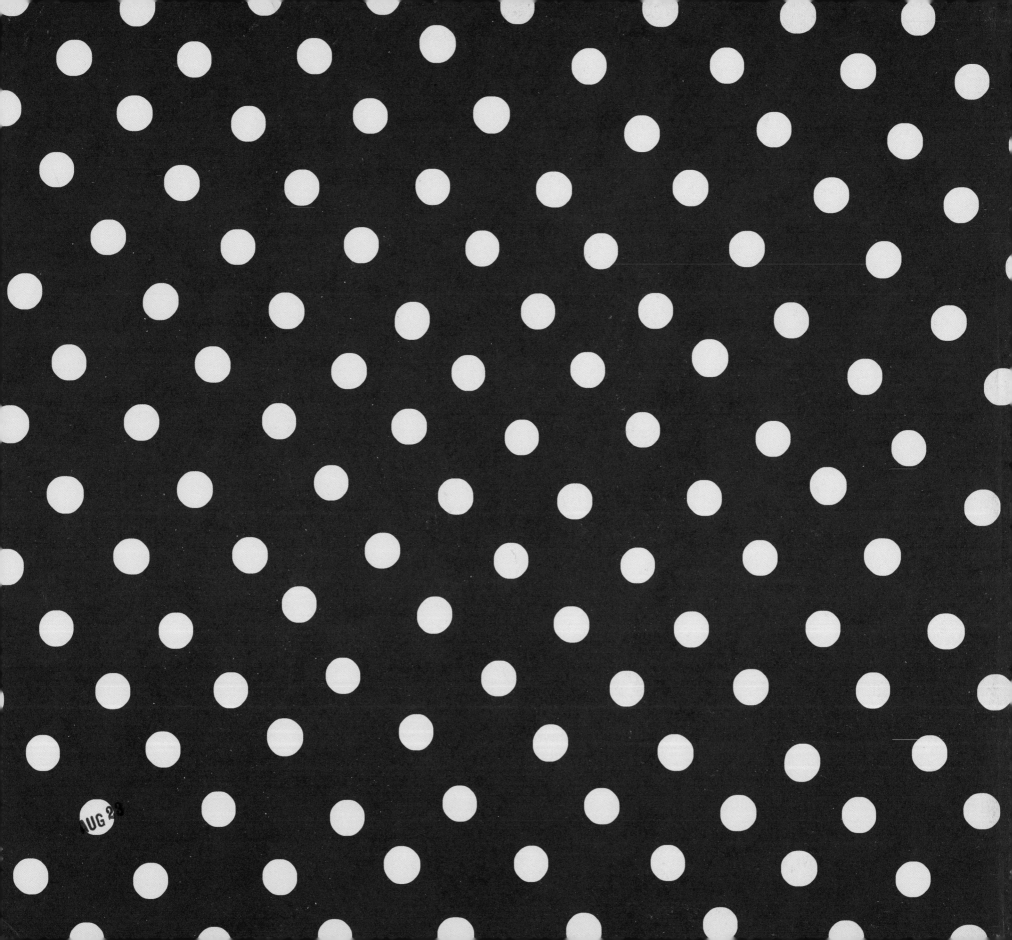